Robert Grant

The Little Tin Gods-On-Wheels or Society in Our Modern Athens

A Trilogy After the Manner of the Greek

Robert Grant

The Little Tin Gods-On-Wheels or Society in Our Modern Athens
A Trilogy After the Manner of the Greek

ISBN/EAN: 9783743383340

Manufactured in Europe, USA, Canada, Australia, Japa

Cover: Foto ©Andreas Hilbeck / pixelio.de

Manufactured and distributed by brebook publishing software
(www.brebook.com)

Robert Grant

The Little Tin Gods-On-Wheels or Society in Our Modern Athens

THE

LITTLE TIN GODS-ON-WHEELS;

OR,

Society in our Modern Athens.

A TRILOGY AFTER THE MANNER OF THE GREEK.

BY ROBERT GRANT.

ILLUSTRATED BY F. G. ATTWOOD.

FROM THE "HARVARD LAMPOON."

SEVENTH EDITION.

CAMBRIDGE:

CHARLES W. SEVER,

UNIVERSITY BOOKSTORE.

1880.

We should not wish to be worldly and beautiful,
Foolish and frivolous.   No, not for anything.

Enter Mr. Carnation *with his opera hat, embossed with a gorgeous
monogram, under his arm.   He scans the various groups with a
troubled air, and then soliloquizes as follows :—*

CARNATION.

O, what a selfish place is this gay world !
Alas ! it wounds me to the quick to see
That ghastly row of unattended maids
Glued, meek as heifers, to the garnished wall.
Shy, shrinking flowers, who but need the sun
Of some man's smile to bloom in peerless beauty ;
And others plain as pikestaffs, but with minds
Cultured and stored with lore of Greece and Rome,
(Ah, what is beauty but a trap and snare,
Unless there is a mind to back it up !)
Around the door a throng of callous brutes,
Who claim the name of men, stand unconcerned
And see these frail exotics droop and wilt
Without a pang, and then go idly home.
Not such am I.   This noble spirit stirs
Me up to action.   I will show these curs
That Chivalry lives still and cannot die.
What ho ! there !   Crocus, will you kindly give me
An introduction to that girl in pink ?

CROCUS.

Great Cæsar's ghost ! . My dear boy, do you know
That that rare maid in pink is she whom men

Who know her style in playful irony
" Old Prob," because she ne'er was known to talk
Of anything but weather, winds, and rain ?
You will be stuck as sure as you are born.
Believe me, I should much prefer to be
" A pagan suckled in a creed outworn,"
Than talk to her.

CARNATION.

Stop, ruthless man! thank Heaven
My heart is not yet hardened by the world.
Poor lamb ! I 'll talk to thee for all thy weather.

CROCUS.

Carnation, in the name of goodness, pause !
Let not your tender nature rule your reason ;
I vow she 's nothing but a mere barometer.

CARNATION.

I swear I 'll speak to her.   Unhand me, Crocus ;
By Heaven! I 'll make mince-meat of him that stops me.

He drags CROCUS *up to* MISS TIGERLILY. CROCUS *introduces him
and immediately leaves.* CARNATION *begins to talk to her in the
most charming and animated way in the background. She replies
languidly.*

CHORUS OF FASHIONABLE YOUNG MEN.

Nothing refineth the young like experience.
He the impetuous, green and undisciplined,
Won't be so eager to talk with that serious-

Minded young damosel after he's been with her
All of an evening, stuck on her terribly.
We the long-suffering, taught by experience,
Foxy as Lucifer, ne'er will be caught again,
Not if we know ourselves, you bet your hat on it!
That is the species of hair-pins that we are!

During the chorus CARNATION *and* MISS TIGERLILY *have approached
the front of the stage. His face, having gradually grown graver
and graver, has now assumed an expression of mingled despair
and horror.*

CARNATION (*having made several attempts at conversation,
tries again*).

You say you do not care for parties much,
You probably have many outside interests?

MISS TIGERLILY.

Yes. Was it raining when you left the street?

CARNATION.

I think it was, but, faith, I did not notice.

MISS TIGERLILY.

What dreadful weather we've been having lately!

CARNATION.

Does not the winter meet your approbation?

MISS TIGERLILY.

I really hardly know. Sometimes I think
That snow is nicest, sometimes I like rain;

Often a thaw delights me, and a freeze
Perhaps is better; pleasant, too, is hail.

Pauses as if frightened at having made such a long speech.

CARNATION (*to change the subject*).

Shall we not try the entry for a change?

MISS TIGERLILY.

No, thank you; I 'll stay here.   I don't like draughts;
I think the wind is high to-night.   I hope
It will go down before the peep of dawn.

CARNATION.

I hope so, truly.   Will you have some supper?

MISS TIGERLILY (*brightening up*).

Yes, thank you; I will take a glass of water,
Some beef, or if there is none, some croquets,
A napkin, and a plate of frozen pudding.

CARNATION *helps her to all these.   She says nothing except that the croquets are too hot and the ice too cold.   Having removed the last plate,* CARNATION *does not return, but moves to the other end of the room, apparently a blighted being.*

CARNATION.

All, all is gone!   The milk of human kindness
Within me is dried up.   Now am I fit
For murder, treason, stratagem, and spoils;
Now could I strangle babes, and smile to see
A cannibal tear beings limb from limb
And roast their joints before a red-hot fire.

I have supped full with horrors, and shall ne'er
Behold it rain or snow without a shudder.
O Crocus, Crocus, I have wronged you deeply!
Straight will I hie me to the foxy caravan
Of youths about the door, and pardon beg
From those whom lately I did so revile.
O, how much sharper than a serpent's tooth
It is to talk to barometric girls!

CARNATION *walks across the room, and shakes* CROCUS'S *hand warmly.*
CROCUS *places a wreath of laurel upon his head, and leads him to the
head of the chorus. Both choruses march about the stage with defiant
gestures.*

CHORUS OF WALLFLOWERS.

See how the ingrate leaves the æsthetic one,
Her the unfortunate, good but not beautiful.
He the illiterate could not appreciate
Her the intelligent.   Men are but simpering
Idiots anyway.   Little she cares for him.
She would not wish to be worldly and beautiful,
Foolish and volatile; no, not for anything.

CHORUS OF FASHIONABLE YOUNG MEN.

See how the prodigal comes to the fold again,
Taught by experience hard, but salubrious.
Sweet is adversity.   He is now disciplined,
Crowned with the laurel, and foxy as Lucifer;
He won't be snared again, not by a jug full!
That is the kind of a hair-pin that he is!

The guests show signs of going home. MISS TIGERLILY *and her mother,
with an injured air, leave the ballroom.* CARNATION *and* CROCUS
*go off arm in arm. The curtain descends while the choruses are
repeating their last strophes.*

THE LITTLE TIN GODS-ON-WHEELS.

A Sequel to " The Wallflowers."

A TRAGEDY AFTER THE MANNER OF THE GREEK.

DRAMATIS PERSONÆ.

MISS JACQUEMINOT, *a raving beauty.*
MISS BONSELLINE, *a tearing bud.*
MR. SOUVENIR, *a howling swell, one of the little Tin Gods-on-Wheels.*
MISS SMILAX, *a parasite.*
Choruses of Tin Gods-on-Wheels, parasitical young ladies, tearing buds, raving beauties, etc.

The scene is laid in Boston, the Modern Athens. The curtain rises on a magnificent ballroom. Young ladies and men of all sorts are grouped about the room. The clock strikes half past ten. The door opens, and MR. SOUVENIR *and a number of other little Tin Gods-on-Wheels just from a dinner-party enter, with boutonnières in their buttonholes and pride in their hearts.*

CHORUS OF LITTLE TIN GODS-ON-WHEELS.

Look at those dear little, sweet little, nice little
Girls in the corner, who are all dying to
Have us come up to them. Which of the darlings
Shall we make happy to-night with our presence ?
We the magnificent leaders of fashion,
Fresh from a dinner and tony as possible ;
We the young men who don't rise in the morning,
Wedded to style, and without occupation.

CHORUS OF PARASITICAL YOUNG LADIES.

Happy the maid whom fate ordains
  To spend the evening with a swell ;
What matter that he has no brains,
  Provided that it looketh well !
For what is sense compared to dog,
  Or intellect to tone and style ?
Though he be heavy as a log,
  If he 's the fashion we will smile.

SOUVENIR, *after gazing around for some moments as if he owned the*
  room, approaches MISS SMILAX, *and offers to shake hands with*
  her in the most patronizing way.

MISS SMILAX.

O Mr. Souvenir ! how nice it is
To see you here.   I had begun to think
You were not coming.   Were you at the dinner ?

SOUVENIR (*gradually edging off*).

Yes.   Charmed, I 'm sure.   Excuse me ; see you later.

By the most skilful manœuvre he slips away before MR. CARNATION,
  the less experienced youth who was talking to MISS SMILAX *when*
  he came up, can anticipate him. MISS SMILAX *beams all over for*
  ten minutes after. SOUVENIR *next approaches* MISS BONSELLINE.

CHORUS OF TEARING BUDS.

Look at that mass of conceited presumption
Going the rounds in his usual manner.
Is n't he horrid ?   But, sisters, speak softly,
It would not do for the world to offend him.
He is a man who can make us or mar us ;

Make us the " thing," or condemn us forever.
So we must smile and seem awfully flattered,
For it is swell to be seen with the creature.
Rough him as much as you like, for he never
By the least possible chance would perceive it ;
For he considers he does us a favor
If he but tread on the train of our dresses.

Souvenir offers his hand to Miss Bonselline very much as if he were Chief Justice of the United States, and she a child of eight. She appears grateful, however.

SOUVENIR.

I hope, Miss Bonselline, you are enjoying
Yourself this evening.   Does the gay world treat you
Kindly, and send you lots of pleasant partners?

MISS BONSELLINE.

O Mr. Souvenir! to have *you* speak to me
Is bliss enough, you know.

SOUVENIR.

O, thank you, thank you!
Don't mention it.   Excuse me ; see you later.

He takes advantage of Mr. Crocus, who has come up to Miss Bonsel- line with a plate of ice-cream, to glide away, although it requires the quickness of a cat, for Crocus has powers that may not be sneezed at, joined to the foxiness of a Nestor. Souvenir next goes up to Miss Jacqueminot, an experienced raving beauty.

CHORUS OF RAVING BEAUTIES.

See how the parasites giggle and flatter,
See how the débutantes smile and look happy,

If he but speak to them, he the time-serving,
Saucy, conceited, and arrogant monster.
Older are we than those volatile damosels ;
We have position, and beaux without number.
But yet (alas for the weakness of woman !)
We still must worship for politic reasons.
He has no brains, to be sure, but his money
Gives him the means to indulge in exotics.
Is there a girl who is proof against roses?
He is a bore of the very first water,
But he gives dinners to those whom he fancies ;
And a club dinner is not to be sneezed at:
Is n't it horrid?　But how can we help it?

SOUVENIR *shakes hands with* MISS JACQUEMINOT *as if he thought that he was doing a charitable act.　She also appears to feel honored.*

SOUVENIR.

Really, Miss Jacqueminot, I 've not been able
To speak to you before ; you 're so surrounded.

MISS JACQUEMINOT.

To have you speak to me at any time
Suffices me ; for beggars can't be choosers.

SOUVENIR.

Ah ! very kind of you to say so, really ; —
There are so many girls it 's quite impossible
To speak to all.　And what with dining out
So much as I do, one gets very weary
Of parties.

MISS JACQUEMINOT.

Yes ; of course a man like you
Must find society grow stale at times ;
Most men of intellect do find it slow.

SOUVENIR.

Yes ; I must own we do.   But I confess
That I am fond of girls ; I really am.

MISS JACQUEMINOT.

O, thank you, thank you !   We are very grateful.

At this moment MR. CARNATION *comes up with a plate of salad.*

SOUVENIR.

Ah ! thank you.   Pray excuse me ; see you later.

SOUVENIR *moves to the other end of the room with a satisfied air.   He
fills a glass with champagne and soliloquizes.* CARNATION *comes up
and listens to him with mouth-open admiration.*

Poor little dears, how much they owe us men !
That girl was almost frantic with delight ;
And those young things with whom I talked at first
Looked proud as peacocks when they had me round.
It wearies one, I know ; but yet it were
A selfish thing to disappoint the dears
By staying e'en a single night at home.
I must be a most fascinating man :
'T is not my fault ; the ladies must blame Heaven.

[*Exit.*

MISS JACQUEMINOT *and* MISS BONSELLINE, *who have been talking together, approach the front of the stage.*

MISS BONSELLINE.

He did ? The horrid, mean, conceited thing !
I never want to speak to him again.

MISS JACQUEMINOT.

Patience, my dear ! To-night we have to smile,
But on the morrow at the sewing-circle
We 'll put a head on this small God-on-Wheels ;
We 'll pick him into little bits of pieces,
And tear his wretched character to rags.
My blood is up at last, and I am fit
For gossip, slander, libel, and revenge.
After this evening's torture I could lie,
Forge, rehypothecate, or play the trick
The adder palmed off on the countryman
Without a pang. O, let us, dearest friend,
From this day forth take pains to make it plain
To man, that woman's never-dying dread
Is talking to a little God-on-Wheels.

*They clasp each other's hands, and move to the head of the united
choruses of tearing buds and raving beauties. MISS SMILAX marches
at the head of the chorus of parasitical girls. The various choruses
begin to move with warlike gestures.*

CHORUS OF PARASITICAL GIRLS.

Happy the maid whom fate ordains
    To pass the evening with a swell !
What matter that he has no brains,
    Provided that it looketh well !
For what is sense compared to dog,
    Or intellect to tone and style ?

Though he be heavy as a log,
If he's the fashion, we all smile.

CHORUS OF LITTLE TIN GODS-ON-WHEELS.

Dear little, sweet little, nice little damosels,
We the magnificent cream of society
Bid you good-night, and we trust you feel gratitude
For the sweet smiles we have scattered among you.
We have been bored, but we gladly put up with it:
Nothing is sweeter than disinterestedness.

CHORUS OF TEARING BUDS AND RAVING BEAUTIES.

See those detestable, time-serving hypocrites,
Probably boasting that we are in love with them.
Pitiful creatures, they think that they flatter us
By their grimaces that look like orang-outang's.
When we assemble to sew for the indigent,
Trust us to tinker the little tin monsters.

The curtain descends while the choruses are still singing.

THE CHAPERONS.

A Supplement to "The Wallflowers" and "The Little Tin Gods-on-Wheels."

A TRAGEDY AFTER THE MANNER OF THE GREEK.

DRAMATIS PERSONÆ.

MR. JACQUEMINOT, *the father of a raving beauty.*
MRS. BONSELLINE, *the mother of a tearing bud.*
MRS. TIGERLILY, *the mother of a wallflower.*
MRS. SOUVENIR, *the mother of a little Tin God-on-Wheels.*
MR. CROCUS, *a worldling of some years' standing.*
MR. SOUVENIR (*fils*), *a howling swell and Tin God.*
MR. CARNATION, *a kind-hearted but inexperienced young man.*

> *Managers of the German.*

Choruses of mothers, fathers, etc.   Various other characters.

The scene is laid in Boston, the Modern Athens.   The curtain rises on a public ballroom.   A German is about to begin.   On seats, around the hall, are ranged a host of Chaperons, mostly mothers and aunts. There are a few fathers scattered among them.   At the door of the dressing-room appear MR. JACQUEMINOT *and daughter,* MESDAMES BONSELLINE, TIGERLILY, SOUVENIR, *with a bevy of their own daughters, and daughters of other people intrusted to them.   The ushers rush forward.* SOUVENIR *secures* MISS JACQUEMINOT.   MR. JACQUEMINOT (*père*) *escorts* MRS. BONSELLINE *to a seat.* CROCUS *leads off* MISS BONSELLINE.   CARNATION *is left to take charge of* MRS. TIGERLILY, *her daughter, and two* MISS DAFFODILS, *from the country, who are staying with* MRS. TIGERLILY.

CHORUS OF CHAPERONS (*mothers*).

We, the mammas of those lovely young damosels,
Once ourselves raving and tearing and beautiful,

We the long-suffering, pitiful chaperons,
Curious, critical, slightly censorious,
Sit here in slumberous, somnolent solitude,
Making remarks, duly tempered with charity,
On the young persons composing society.
See that unfortunate Eleanor Daffodil,
Fresh from the country, and green as asparagus.
Look at the cut and the set of the dress on her,
Does n't she have the effect of a rag-bag?
Taste never ran in the Daffodil family.

MRS. SOUVENIR (*conversing with* MR. JACQUEMINOT).

O Mr. Jacqueminot, your lovely daughter
Looks like a queen to-night; that perfect dress,
Which came from Worth, — I know it by the cut, —
Is truly exquisite. My Alice Blanche
Comes out next winter, and I really think
That I shall send to him for all her clothes.

MR. JACQUEMINOT.

Your daughter, Mrs. Souvenir, would captivate
In any dress. Her laughing, liquid eyes
Will shatter hearts like reeds. I hear your son
Is *so* attractive; only watch him now,
With what a finished air of well-bred ease
He 's fanning Lulu Bonselline. O, charming, charming!

MRS. TIGERLILY (*to* MRS. BONSELLINE, *seated on the other side of the room*).

Tell me, my dear, who made that lovely tulle
Of Lulu's? It must surely be Pingard's.

MRS. BONSELLINE.

No, it was made by Felix, and it fits
Extremely well, and yet upon the whole   ·
I think that Froment gives more satisfaction,
He trims so sweetly.   It is such a comfort
To get one's things in Paris ; such a contrast
In prices to the wretches on this side,
Although I must confess that Santin made
A bonnet for my Lulu, that compares
With Virot's very well.

MRS. TIGERLILY.

My Georgiana
Finds Parcher pretty good.   O dear, O dear !
I said it would be so !   Look how her skirt
Is hanging !   Tell me, dear, what shall I do ?

*Makes frantic signs to her daughter, who finally approaches on the
arm of* CARNATION.   MRS. T. *whispers to her, and she goes off to
the dressing-room, while* CARNATION *waits for her at the door.*

CHORUS OF CHAPERONS (*mothers*).

Don't you believe that it 's pretty near supper-time ?
We are beginning to get up an appetite,
Silently sitting in slumberous solitude.
Look how that volatile little Miss Bonselline 's
Torn all to tatters her train irreproachable,
Dancing that horrible, barbarous redowa.
Watch that unfortunate youngest Miss Daffodil
Try to keep time with the elegant Souvenir !
O, what a bungle and mess she has made of it !

CARNATION *brings some salad and champagne to* MRS. TIGERLILY
and MRS. BONSELLINE. SOUVENIR *comes up in a very magnificent
manner after they are helped, and asks if he can get them anything.*

MRS. TIGERLILY.

O, thank you, no, we have got all we want :
Your party is a wonderful success.

SOUVENIR *bows his thanks, waves his opera hat superbly, and glides
away.*

He certainly has most delightful manners.
That young Carnation is a real good boy,
But rather *gauche*, you know.   O, there's my Georgy
Talking to Hurly Crocus !   Don't they make
A charming couple ?

MRS. BONSELLINE.

Very much so, dear.
But, O, do tell me who is that strange man
That's talking now to Peepy Jacqueminot?

MRS. TIGERLILY.

Why, he's a titled Englishman, named Nightshade,
Spending a fortnight with young Scarlet Runner.
Lord Deadly Nightshade's what I think they call him.
They say he's awful rich and full of talent.

MRS. BONSELLINE.

How nice ! now really, you don't tell me so ?
Why, just look there, he's being introduced
To Lulu, — O, I hope she'll have the sense
To ask him to our party.   Is it not

A most distinguished name, — Lord Deadly Nightshade?
It 's dangerous to have a handsome daughter.

MRS. TIGERLILY.

I feel with you, my dear, I 've just found out
That Georgy is a beauty.   Only think,
Cecilia Mignonette told Martha Cowslip
That Mr. Jacqueminot told her that Georgy
Had finer eyes than any girl in Boston.
He is a first-rate judge, and lots of others
Have told me the same thing.   I 've always thought
Her quite nice-looking, but, dear, nothing further.
I see a mother's judgment can't be trusted.
You ought to see her in her new spring kilt,
Cut very short ; she really does look sweetly.

MRS. SOUVENIR (*to* MR. JACQUEMINOT).

Just do look now at Georgy Tigerlily
Sitting alone, — she 's never taken out.
One would suppose her mother would get tired
Of seeing her neglected.   But she goes
Night after night, and says that she enjoys it.
Poor child ! it is not her fault that she 's plain.

MR. JACQUEMINOT.

She has not certainly a ray of beauty,
No style, and Peepy says no conversation.

MRS. SOUVENIR.

O, what a contrast she is to your Peepy !

MR. JACQUEMINOT *whispers something in reply that is inaudible.*
MRS. SOUVENIR *looks immensely flattered.*

CHORUS OF CHAPERONS (*fathers*).

Look here now, we are decidedly sick of this ;
It 's the last time that we mean to put up with it,
Sitting up this way till two in the morning !
One must be made like the Archangel Gabriel,
Blessed with Job's patience, and more than humanity
Not to get mad at this wildly preposterous,
Perfectly scandalous state of society.
When we were young would our parents have winked at it ?
Not they, the sturdy and strait-laced old Puritans !
We will not either, and this is the last of it, —
This is the last of it, you bet your hat on it !

CHORUS OF CHAPERONS (*mothers*).

Come, dears, it 's time to be putting an end to it,
We are all getting as sleepy as pussy-cats.
Lulu must be up all fresh for her practising
Early to-morrow, and Peepy has harmony.
O, it is hard on us pitiful chaperons,
Sitting alone in our slumberous solitude.
O, we are somnolent !   Where are the carriages ?
Wrap yourselves well, dears, the night is a chilly one.
Once *we* were charming and lovely young damosels,
Once *we* were raving and tearing and beautiful.

The party breaks up. MISS TIGERLILY *and* MISS BONSELLINE
shake and wake their respective mothers. MR. JACQUEMINOT, *in a
jaded manner, sees* MRS. SOUVENIR *to the dressing-room door. The
ushers rush after hacks. The curtain descends while the choruses are
still singing.*

OXYGEN!

A MT. DESERT PASTORAL.

OXYGEN !

A MT. DESERT PASTORAL.

A trifle offered by Lampy without comment, as an example of the effect that a bracing atmosphere can produce upon conservative natures.

DRAMATIS PERSONÆ.

MISS ALICE BUNTING, *of Philadelphia, ætatis* 21 *yrs.* 6 *mos.*
MR. ARTHUR FLANNELSHIRT, A. B., LL. B., *of Boston, ætatis* 26 *yrs.* 3 *mos.*

SCENE I. — *Mt. Desert.   Corridor of Rodick House. Hour,* 10.30 *P. M.*

Enter MISS BUNTING *and* MR. FLANNELSHIRT *arm in arm. Her dress is a blue and white boating-suit, cut short. A hat with a huge brim and draped with a large red handkerchief is perched on the back of her head. He is attired in a gray shirt of flannel, a pair of patched pantaloons, a skullcap, and canvas shoes. He is smoking a pipe. She pauses at room twenty, and taking a key from her pocket gives it to him. He unlocks the door. She goes in and returns with a small pitcher.*

ALICE.

AND now, good night.   But ere you go, do get me,
As usual, some hot water from the kitchen.

ARTHUR.

Give me the jug, and in half a jiffy
I will be back.   (*Runs down the corridor.*)

ALICE (*shrieking after him*).

Be sure that it is boiling!

She goes into her room and shuts the door. Interval of five minutes. Re-enter ARTHUR, *with the pitcher of hot water and a plate of hard crackers. He knocks, and she puts her head out.*

ALICE.

What made you take so long?   But O, how lovely,
To bring me some hard crackers too!   Just toss me
One from the plate and see if I can catch it.

He does so, and she, emerging from the room, tries to catch it in her mouth. The cracker falls on the ground. They both stoop to pick up the pieces, and bump their heads.

ALICE.

You horrid thing!   You stupid, awkward creature!
     She playfully flings the bits of cracker at him.

ARTHUR.

Come now, it's much too early to retire.
Let's go and eat our crackers on the staircase ;
It would be sort of weird.   Say, don't you think so ?

ALICE.

Why, yes.   I think it would be quite romantic !
You really can't imagine what a comfort
It is to have no matron to annoy one,
To dog one's steps and harp on what is proper !
A girl that's civilized don't need a matron.

Thank Heaven, father let me come without one.
He kicked at first, but by judicious treatment
I brought him round. I 'm ready now, if you are.

*They proceed to the staircase and sit down on the top stair, with the
water-pitcher between them.*

ALICE (*munching crackers*).

O, ain't this jolly, it is so informal !
Why, only think, we two set out together
At nine this morning to explore and ramble.
We 've spent the day together on the mountain,
And never parted once.   The heat of noontide
Found us companions still, and evening's shadow
Saw you and me without a person near us.
Where else, but here, could we do this without
Exciting comment?

ARTHUR.

　　　　　　　Nowhere, sad to mention.
In Boston, where I live, if I should happen
To walk twice with some fascinating creature
I should dead certain be reported smitten,
Engaged, and when that turned out false, rejected.
But here, to pass the day with whom you want to, —
Pass two days, three days, four days, even five days,
In the society of girls one fancies,
Is not regarded as the least peculiar.
What do you say, now, to a row by moonlight?

ALICE.

The very thing!   O, what a boon is freedom!

They rise from the stairs.   She goes to her room and gets a shawl, which he tenderly puts over her shoulders.   Arm in arm they go down, leaving the pitcher in the middle of the staircase.

SCENE II. — *Bar Harbor.   Mt. Desert.*

A row-boat is floating on the tranquil water.   A nearly full moon is high in the heavens.   She is stretched out in the stern.   He slowly paddles with the oars.   Several other boats can be seen in the distance, but not near enough to distinguish the parties.

ALICE.

This is a first-rate place to get acquainted ;
Day before yesterday I 'd never seen you,
And now I feel as if I 'd known you ages.

ARTHUR.

In my prim city, I might live next door to
A girl for ten years, and not know her nearly
As well as I know you.   This comes of freedom!
Look at those boats on this side and on that side,
Each freighted with two other kindred spirits,
More intimate, perhaps, than even we are.
They probably have rambled weeks together,
And rowed upon the water every evening.
This beats the New Republic all to hollow;
Paul and Virginia were nothing to it.

ALICE.

If I were at Nahant, Cohasset, Newport,
Or any other of those horrid places,
I should be forced in cold blood to abandon
This blessed moon, and go to bed when pa did.
But, fortunately, Mrs. Easy-Going,
Who promised pa to keep an eye upon me,
Don't care a button what I do, provided
I do not interfere with her Amelia,
Who spends her time with little Peter Minestock.
I hope she 'll get him, but I pity Peter !

By way of variety, she gives him a playful spatter with the oar. He laughs, and spatters her back. He proposes to anchor, and she acquiesces. She stretches herself out in the stern, he in the bow, with a pipe.

ALICE.

Now, ain't this lovely, to be so devoted !
It 's twenty times as good as an engagement,
Because we know that, if we ever happen ·
To weary of each other, we have only
To part, and cotton to another person, —
You to some girl, and I to some new fellow.

ARTHUR.

I could spend·years with you and never weary !

ALICE.

Don't be too sure.   You 're merely a spring chicken,
And I have practised at this thing four summers.

You will get sick of me before a fortnight
Is ended.

ARTHUR.

Never, O, believe me, never;
I ne'er have seen a girl that I admired,
Adored, respected, loved, and venerated
So much as I do you.

ALICE.

What perfect nonsense !
What would your ma say ?   O, young man, be careful;
All Philadelphians are not like me, sir !
Nine out of ten would snap you up directly
For words like those, and marry you before you
Could count Jack Robinson !

ARTHUR.
O lovely being !
I 'm thine forever, if you only say so.
For all I care, my ma may go to glory.

ALICE.

How sweet to be thus loved !   No more at present,
I will reflect on what you say.   It 's time now
To go to bed.   What hour says your repeater ?

ARTHUR.
'T is half past twelve.

ALICE.

'T is sad to part, but needful.

They slowly get to rights and haul up the anchor. She takes the oars and rows towards the shore; he puffs his pipe pensively.

SCENE III. — *The Corridor of the Rodick House. Hour,* 1.15 *A. M.*

They re-enter arm in arm. Somebody has stepped on and upset the pitcher during their absence. After a few minutes' conversation he goes and gets some more boiling water.

ALICE (*going into her room*).

And now, once more, good night.

ARTHUR.

To-morrow morning
I 'll come at nine.

ALICE (*sticking her head out*).

All right, I shall be ready,
And we will spend the day again together,
As usual to our mutual satisfaction.
We 'll climb, read poetry, drive, row, loaf, and ramble
From morn to dewy eve, and I will teach you
The latest dodge in scientific flirting ;
Giving you points, and Heaven knows you need them !
You 'll be an adept by this time next summer,
If you don't let such stuff as that you uttered
To night destroy the fruits of my good teaching.

But when, in future days, you are distinguished
For being able with your little finger
To set the heart of any girl a beating,
And not to care a rush, say that I taught you.
Say, " Alice Bunting, a sweet Philadelphian,
A maiden unaffected and spontaneous,
Who always did exactly what she wanted,
And went from principle without a matron,
Found me a callow youth, a perfect chicken,
And made me what I am. — Be hers the glory."
Good night, good night! Remember, nine to-morrow.

Kisses her hand to him, and closes the door.

ARTHUR.

Good night, good night! O, why ain't more girls like her!

Walks slowly and pensively down the corridor.

www.ingramcontent.com/pod-product-compliance
Lightning Source LLC
Chambersburg PA
CBHW020818030726
47496CB00009B/2946